A Bleeding in Black Leather

John Pietaro

UnCollected Press

A BLEEDING IN BLACK LEATHER

Cover Art:

John Pietaro
Still Selby's Brooklyn
photography collage with found imagery

Back Cover Artwork:

John Pietaro
Jack Always Knew
Photography

Author Photo: **Laurie Towers**

Book Design by:

UnCollected Press
8320 Main Street, 2nd Floor
Ellicott City, MD 21043

For more books by UnCollected Press:
www.therawartreview.com

First Edition 2022
ISBN: [ISBN]

CONTENTS

For Laurie,
as is my every effort and achievement of tenacity, pride and creativity

This book is also dedicated to New York City at night, its streets, its rivers, steel canyons and broken sky, its downtown, galleries, bars and bookstores, and its denizens of the dark.

We, all of us, are its night people.

"Taste the whip, in love not given lightly"

-Lou Reed

"They'll mark with a cross of blood, every house, every door"

-Bertolt Brecht

"The burning witch, her mouth covered by leather to strangle her words"

-Margaret Atwood

"With their souls of patent leather, they come down the road. Hunched and nocturnal"

-Federico Garcia Lorca

"The blood jet is poetry; there is no stopping it"

-Sylvia Plath

"Poetry's always dead"

-Richard Hell

"Writing is easy. Just sit down at your typewriter and bleed"

-Ernest Hemingway

"You did thirst for blood, and with blood I fill you"

-Dante Alighieri

The Night Leonard Cohen Died

Subway ride from Brooklyn seemed nothing short of average.

Subway ride from Brooklyn deemed nothing more of average, but then, yet then, I --

I misjudged how far east I'd land.

That was odd, surely odd in itself, as I'd traveled to 23rd Street many times before. But on this night, November's grey going black, nothing was settled and nothing familiar up from under. It was just one of those things, one of those odd things tired travelers sometimes experience in

Closed, crowded places.

Once street-level, after hitting the nearest corner, I slowed my pace considerably. "Hell", I thought, "I'm walking in the wrong direction." Awkwardly stopping at a newsstand, though needing nothing, no paper, no cigarettes, nothing, just biding moments, I gazed blankly over the rows of candy. *"Yeah...?"* newsstand guy looked through me as he chewed something. Buying a roll of peppermints,

I walked back over my same steps, aimed due west.

On to 5th Avenue. At the light, I opened the mints and regretted not getting wintergreen. It was an oddly warm night, recalling early September. 6th Avenue came, went, then 7th.

Recalling early September, though inordinately dark;

The clouded starlessness a blue-black as I strolled up the street.

And a crowd had gathered in front of

The Chelsea Hotel.

Candles lined the sidewalk casting a shimmer, revealing flowers of mournful white. I slowly approached the building and saw a large black-and-white photo bathed in vigil. “Suzanne” played softly on a portable stereo as the crowd blankly milled about.

“I still can’t believe he’s gone”, one within whispered to another. I stepped, then, into the tribute for a fallen poet, becoming one with my own lamentation.

Tri-colored the clouds, autumn rains traverse, these

Droplets in pictures upon dampened grounds. With

Sky surging black, clocks chimed in reverse,

Recalling youth, the most restless of sounds.

Listen well, loudly; can you quite hear?

A roiling and rumbling from just behind,

It breathed out in song, echoing years.

It locked in my pulse, a throbbing of time.

Electric the blue, the bellows sang past as

I walked the stones beneath orbs of red.

Up flights of marble, the reverb was cast

In spandex and sweat the building unshed.

The ripples were spied as I turned away.

A peel of the bells, timepiece recall,

From the near sacred to utmost urbane,

It’s there for the want, the dusk of a pall.

As trembles below claim amity's bliss,
A rush on the tracks to feed center stage.
Scent of the burn as shadows conflict
The wind of what's lost to a much younger age.

Till sounds of the pass fall tacit with tire and
Call of the flowers douse shadows below,
A sizzling and flaming of everyday pyre melt
Clockface, the taming of memories remote.

-May 28, 2021, 1:52 AM

A Bleeding in Black Leather

The air restrains our mid-August fever,
Contained hungrily, of greed and vice in
The near-cool of night.
First Avenue dreams, though restlessly so,
During what now passes for
The after-hours.

Poets moan of downtown past, yet,
The Village hasn't been
Since Cobweb Hall went dark and the
Bohemians outed by prying eyes.
Provincetown played Reed, O'Neill, and Millay but
Mabel Dodge shuttered her salon when
Emma was deported and Jack left for Baku.

Art was a weapon, the masses anew, and
Café Society bristled in blue.
"Strange Fruit" hung over Sheridan Square, as
Daily, workers shouted for
Freedom From Want, Freedom From Fear and
Woody and Pete sang Songs for John Doe,
Cultural the rebel, the seer entombed,

The Beats, grown in Village war-time womb

Where Burroughs at Chumley's walked Kerouac's road.

Ginsberg went west, crying out Howl,

As kettles of fish drained Minetta Lane,

Hemingway's booze still stoned Le Metro.

Remember, Bird's wings went bare at Camarillo, missing the sky as

Tompkins called revelry, dire breadth of Anthropology.

But Monk wouldn't stop to see, Brilliant be the

Corners in colors he cast.

A glass in each hand, he danced from the Vanguard to

Far, very far away.

Candle-lit that numbing June, weary the tears fell upon Union Square,

As crimes of the mind melted 60 Centre. Paradise the Alley.

Coltrane, the sheets of shadows in despair.

Calling out A and 11th, subterranean, oh,

Yes, and Umbra,

LeRoi saw Hughes at the 5-Spot and took on the Cedar,

With and without Di Prima

(who shouted out midtown bold).

His *Floating Bear* with Hettie cast hysterics in Bureau-speak:

Journals of journals of struggles be told.

Ornette and de Koonig forged Bowery mystique but

The lofts birthed by Sun Ra,

Closet high-modern oblique.

O'Hara, and Joans, Corso and Waldman magnetized blackened skies.

And Ayler, well before the wading, cried out new blues, heart of raw

As the Eye Peace Bookstore and pubes of poets offended decenctly.

Nascent Fugs killed for piece, yodeling yippie.

Ginsberg cried foul through ballads of morrow

Decrying censors and curfews of Washington Square.

Draft card embers greyed our spring, yet how many

How many weren't marching? Anymore. War over war. All sorrow,

Over now, baby…burning, baby, burning, surging, burning as

Baraka moved north, stare down the Man and Newport, too,

Reclaiming the music, reclaiming, renaming the turning. Burning.

And then Stonewall boiled……

Queen and hippy, bastard sons harkening,

Grey flannel 'neath Woodstock rainbow fading

As Warhol lay on Fact'ry floor bleeding.
But horse, thought to race away the vagrancy,
Brought in the business, ghettoed the rest, and the
Poetry church redeemed all but the global Piss Factory.

The echoes will whisper of
Sweet Jane and roses, and
Street love in spurts,
Singe of echo bays on.
Left hand's embrace fingers exaltation,
A rise of the moon and
Sediment's reprise.

Scent of sweat lives on in leather,
Buckle browned with rust.
Cave drippings at CBs, puddles onstage,
Sizzling the leads and flaming reverb;
Silver the sound, See/Hear the soul,
Razor to ear, severing weight of
No Wave gold.

As artists sang gospel on Alphabet's cusp,
La Mama, No Rio deflected the nouveau,

Crist'dora reflected "Die Yuppie Scum".

Stockbrokers and whores bent down for ACT-UP.

The riots were time, tempting old valor;

Masked with religion,

A prayer for the bomb.

One with night air, repelled by miasma,

Eyes seek only the route to revealed.

And nothing was left of tarantula's dancing,

Just relieving, the letting,

The straying afield.

Pulse drumming divisions shout out the silence,

Distortion of passion and amplified steel.

- June 13, 2021, 11:32 PM

Thrown Shadows

Almost 6:50 PM, thickening gray above as the sky faded black. Eyelids heavy, the drive home felt particularly long, the traffic abnormally aggravating. Every hesitant driver was now lined up in front of his car, funereal. This would be less ironic if not for the company within: those persistent cadences of the past.

They spoke to him, wavering between the dash and rear windshield.

Without saying anything. The chatter, like probing headlight glare, was unavoidable.

Who would have expected this tenacity from such a lowly haunt?

Jack finally left the car, too tired for concern with the parking ticket come morning, walking heavily toward his building as rain fell over head and shoulders. "Goddamn, it couldn't have waited a few more minutes…", he thought, dragging himself leaden.

Once inside, no time was wasted in getting upstairs and into bed. Rainfall tapped steady time on the window as a cloud-obscured moon gilt the blinds.

Jack's reddened eyes scanned the room cautiously.
And then he was asleep.

Memories chased in painted fog pouring over his dreamscape. A rainfall of imagery rolled down heads and shoulders and grounds. Clocks chimed in reverse as he landed in 1981, back in college. And the soundtrack faded into a restless bassline roiling, chafing, but furtively so, his pulse locking into strut tempo.

His hair was longer then, so now it thickened and lengthened accordingly, just as the trim beard was not very credible back when, so now wiped clean. From the depths of REM, he walked the grassy path of an uncertain campus.

Background music morphed into Laurie Anderson, heavy reverb and repetition, with excerpts of early Blondie B-sides added in.

Blue light of Ornette on a Saturday night hanged into *The Ascension*, living in bushes of ghosts in captures by Dial-a-Poem. Please deposit 10 cents more for the next three minutes…

He walked. This seemed familiar, but then nothing is truly familiar in dreams, especially with the clouds bathed in camouflage. After suffering through blue-collar high school, where the toughs all thought they were John Travolta, dancing while beating you up, graduation had signaled escape. He'd insisted on going to the best out-of-state arts college to study playwrighting, poetry and that new thing folks were calling performance art.

"One Night in Bangkok" echoed from somewhere remote.
Murray Head, a video star whose name was never recalled
during wake hours, orated on in a blur of echo.
It sounded cobalt blue.

Best laid plans and all that. As it turned out, Jack ended up at the nearby junior college in Brooklyn's Manhattan Beach. Other than the name, the area had less to do with Manhattan than any other part of Brooklyn. Sounded sexy but the water was actually part of Sheepshead Bay. He later transferred to a local senior college. No dorms, no out-of-state experiences and not a lot of underground theatre. Of course, the downtown subway was never too far off.

The specter of *Saturday Night Fever* hung over Brooklyn like a sparkling disco ball, just as it throbbed up and down every major thoroughfare. From speeding Cadillacs with bass-boost speakers driven by guys named Cheech in blown D.As and half-buttoned shirts for the thick necks and gold chains. The strange language they spoke, a rendering of De Niro-strewn Brooklynese festered with a marble-mouthed deformity, was understood by few. It has since fallen from the vernacular, much like conversational Latin.
And yet, those voices cling to the walls in Marley fades.

Apparitions.

"Hey, Jack! Jack-- we need to get in another band practice". That, however, was a welcome voice emerging from the wings. "Those songs from *London Calling* aren't going to come together if we don't rehearse".

Coming into view was Craig, Craig Osborn-Greene. Dyed blonde hair shorn into a Mohawk, contrasting against a dark brown complexion. Craig wore his standard motorcycle leathers sporting anti-Reagan and anti-Thatcher pins, the anarchy "A", and some of the little square punk album pins, too. On his back he wore a guitar, a red, headless Steinberger knock-off; he liked carrying it out like that. Craig stood over 6-feet, had bulging arms and wore ear cuffs and safety pins. No one touched the ax.

Jack looked down and saw that the schoolbooks he'd been carrying were now transferred to a backpack slung over one shoulder, and the object weighing down his right hand had become a guitar in leatherette case. He'd bought it used at Big Barry's Music House two years earlier. The instrument had called out to him from its stand in the shop's window. A sparkling black Telecaster with black pickguard he'd adorned with a hammer and sickle affixed under layers of lacquer. And to be sure the message was certain, Jack painted across the front what Woody Guthrie had stated on his guitar: *This Machine KILLS Fascists.* 'Left Populist Punk', they called it.

Jack and Craig had been running ads in *the Village Voice, NY Rocker* and *Trouser Press* for months, searching for the right bassist and drummer. They'd finally found the bassist, even if the drummer proved more elusive.

Klara "Frozen" Rosen was a student at Brooklyn College who played her clear plexiglass bass with a throbbing edge and sang in a shrill wail. A feminist who looked to smash the patriarchy, the pink and black spiked hair belied her Wall Street plans. Any more serious about music, she'd never have settled for this band.

As Jack and Craig walked the grassy row, the baroque entrance to the Liberal Arts Building somehow led into the soundproofed doorway of Human Fly Rehearsal Studios. Looking over his shoulder, as the door shut, Jack peered onto shadowy Stillwell Avenue, just under the elevator train tracks, the scent of Coney Island Beach and Perfume Bay equally present. They entered Room 1 and the buzzsaw of Frozen's bass shook the large amplifier cabinets and both young men were now at microphones, wearing their guitars, mid-song. The Clash's "Spanish Bombs" with Jack adding stray Burroughs readings.

The trio played on, and there entered Elliot Steinmann. Though he had no experience as a band manager, he posed in this role quite believably and his background as a jazz club owner in both Paris and Morocco carried a luster. He'd worked with the greats of the 1950s and '60s. He said. And loved saying it. "Thelonious Monk was a rare genius", he'd often explain, "but so introverted that one could barely touch him. Like a rare flower, he was a gift to the world that came briefly, and then would be gone."

As he lectured through a learned, slowly enunciated old Delancey Street accent, Elliot offered bits of wisdom, breaking into French as the mood struck, adding in philosophic quotes and segments of poetry without cause. They cherished him.

"You guys have a rare quality, too. The three of you, even without the drummer, carry that beat into tomorrow. It's unique, kids, unique". Elliot looked up at them from the old couch in the corner of the room, staring dramatically through tinted glasses and locks of thick, white hair trickling over his forehead, combed like Kerouac. One can imagine that as a young man, he either wanted to be Kerouac or to make love to him.

"And did I ever tell you about the Modern Jazz Quartet? It was my idea to use that name!" As he railed on about the efficacy of modernism, the back wall of the studio momentarily evaporated into the supermarket where Jack worked after school. Just as the cash register was about to replace his guitar, Elliot stood and motioned dramatically.

“First thing: you guys gotta get a name”, he said, pulling on his index finger. “I tell you this, like, every day. Where the hell would the Beatles be today if they weren’t known as the Beatles? I’ve offered you, uh, the Robots of Death (now tugging on his middle finger). And then there was Death Be Not Proud (ring finger) and my take-off on Mailer, the Naked and the Undead (pinky). And my particular favorite, the Death Knells”, he said, pointing individually to each of the three over each of the words. “I keep sayin’ it—write a song called “Hell’s Bells” and you can’t go wrong if you’re the Death Knells”.

Removing his glasses for effect, Elliot said, “I will order business cards from that printer on Avenue X the minute you settle on a name. I know the guy and he’ll do a rush!”.

Elliot also spoke to them about showmanship though Frozen had no desire to wear electrical tape over her nipples instead of a shirt. “Forget it, I’m not gonna be Naked so they can be the Undead, Elliot!”, she snorted. Privately, he complained that this was the frigid in Frozen.

A long tacit as the scent of carnations seemed to fill the room.

“Do you know the technical difference between a hobo, a bum and a tramp?”, Elliot interrupted as they were counting off another number. After some moments of blank stares, Elliot continued, with deliberation. “A hobo travels, seeking work. A tramp travels and sometimes seeks work. And a bum stays local and never seeks work.

“There is a pecking order in every social strata”.

The carnations were gone.

Fade to white.

Night for Day: 11 of 9

The sky.
Its relentless grip on night
And weary seizure of moons, the
Smoked gray face stared down upon us, a
Saw-toothed cobalt on high.

Straight till morning it held, this
Night for day, night for day
When few could speak and the
City, too, soared long past gone.
Yet, the spheres repulsed.

Barely shaven, early risers gazed
As market trolled for dawn,
The apparition of time,
Annulling the unseen.
Traversing decades.

It turned bitter, then, the cold,
Though day now for day.
Inner halls framed hollowed eyes and
We came of the pitch,

All nether extolled.

Nothing spoke but the buildings,
Just fit for the breaching.
Sky's entrails, so wicked the light,
Its face unfurled
In naked exhibition.

Sang torrid air,
Wind over wind and
Night for night, 'til
The hours conceded
In dire contraire.

Too much sediment to commit,
Our clouded earth fallen,
Unchaste and astray,
Sailed in repose and
Fell far, so far from remit.

-Feb 27, 2021, 1:35am

-For all we've lost-

***Pre-Dawn Morning** – for Lou Reed*

Velveteen the sun, too far to touch,

Distant star.

Shards of light carve the turn of rhythm and

Most lucent tempo.

Unexpected the harmonies about his voice,

Leatherette of tone, severing mere emotion.

Sweet, the edge, as pulsations carry the streaming,

Infected pathway, bitter the blood.

And then, by turn, the voices chant,

Call of protest and darkest surrender.

Over the hill now, or so he claimed,

At least for the hour.

See: late summer storms cutting the grooves and

Slicing the inevitable umbilical.

Oh, Brookdale, it's haunted wards and

Shadows of streets melt into waves,

56 Ludlow, 222 West 23rd, lonely

Highway and uptown subway,

Station's corners quell the moment,

Revealing the blackest shades, the iron ore,

The howl of Quine, dance of Saunders,

The hands of Anderson, heart of Lulu.

His foray, poetic sound, came,

Colored only with the pre-dawn morning.

-September 2, 2021, 10:23pm

Stand, Sonny

Sonny, Sonny,
Sonny standing at the bridge,
Sonny, Sonny Boy,
Man, man of many men.
Dancing through his hands,
Fingers astray,
Liberate!
Of mind that they
Shredding what was.
Stand Sonny,
Sonny, Stand.

Dark Midnight, Oxford tone,
Blackest-blue,
The bird already flew to
Paths unknown,
Improvisationally free.
Dum-dum-dap,
Dum-dum-dap,
Dum-dum-de-dum-dum-ber-dum
Dum-dum-de-dap!

Streams of this and

Oceans that;

Phrasing, phrasing, phraseology,

Catch me, catch me,

Oh, Colossus,

St. Thomas,

Saint This or Daemon That,

And old cow hands,

Babs and Bud, Fats, Miles and Monk,

Max and Brownie

Stand, Sonny,

Sonny stand.

Clarinet in newsprint,

Carried in hand,

Choco the sound, no matter

No matter the land.

Stand Sonny, stand,

Freedom banned.

Sonny, Sonny, oh,

Sonny stand!

Flatbush Avenue, June 19, 2020, 6:19PM
-For Sonny Rollins and Juneteenth-

Those Enduring Neon Moments

He breathed out, long and wide, leaning into the lateness. And then he let go. Mid-summer's stillness reached triumphantly through the open window just as his laptop sliced the deep dark blue. Staring for a moment at his now empty, open hand, Mike peered down between the quivering fingers to follow the descent; the thing, still partially open, expressed a certain awareness through its lighted screen. It rotated twice in mid-air before careening the remainder of the fourteen-story drop, traveling with a gentleness, gliding downward, bathed in soft night air.

Well after 2AM, it was, and his eyes ached. Following the path of decline, his vision swooned into an unfocused field of blacks and grays. As devoid of clarity as had been his writing all night long. And as the tiny, silvery blur struck bottom, the eruption in violent, shattering bounces spilled upward and then back down several times. It seems unlikely, but he would later claim that the crushing impact produced a brief but enticing rainbow of electronic fireworks in the dark, shimmering and dancing over West 87th Street in digital reds, yellows and blues. And the goddamned thing actually screamed in terror, he insisted, anticipating the rapidly oncoming sidewalk.

Thriving in this rare moment of satisfaction after fifteen anguished months of publishers' rejections and then having an agent not just quit, but actually fire *him*, Mike shut the window, decidedly clicking the lock behind it. He laid back on the sofa, drinking in the air-conditioned atmosphere, committed to giving the act no further import. With a hand over his forehead and into the graying hair, he slowly fell into a sleep that blocked all colors shimmering in the night. Any dreams would have to emerge in a rich black-and-white, rotating slowly in the damp air of very early morning.

He was eight years old. Again. The third grade.

It was a Friday evening so he could stay up late.

'The Million Dollar Movie' was set to show a film he'd never heard of before; something called *A Thousand Clowns*. Mom, a room away, was sitting in the kitchen with her friend Tilly. Dad was out, so for once little Mike had reign of the family television set.

A Thousand Clowns. What a cool title. Maybe it was something about the circus. He flipped the TV to channel 9 and sat on the floor just in front of it. As the program began, the small screen came alive with Manhattan's cityscape painted in scenic, enduring neon. Jack could smell the coffee perking as Mom cut into the crumb cake.

Bits of conversation streamed in from the kitchen, but he was focused on the RCA console, 20th century's family hearth.

Taxi headlights tossed beams through the evening rush, the Empire State Building, Broadway, Lincoln Center, Sardi's and the spectacles of midtown aglow in electric postmodern light-streams.

What could be more alluring, especially from far-off Brooklyn? New York at night, a quivering, glittering land mass in micro-tonal polychrome,

blooming in blackness like the mariphasa lupine lumina.

Everything, all at once, in a few spare moments.

Music he would later realize was from *Gone with the Wind* emoted from the solid-state cabinet, filling the room with lush sound before the announcer assured that the film

would begin...

No circus tale, *A Thousand Clowns* is the story of Murray Burns, a singularly bohemian writer, breathed to life by Jason Robards. After abruptly quitting his job scripting a ridiculous children's program, Murray basks in his joblessness—his very nonconformity is the heart of the character—but eventually must face his lack of responsibility toward the young nephew he is raising and the bills he must pay. The film faithfully adapted from Herb Gardner's 1962 play was a fascinating study of a creative living in what was then a low-rent district--since gone the way of every gentrified community. Shot in many Manhattan locations, uptown and down, interspersed with ersatz crowd scenes powered by Sousa marches and Murray's propensity toward shouting early-morning insults to New York's wealthy, Mike was enthralled. *What was this thing Murray is...a writer?* The imagery was already solidly packed into his mind's eye.

- "Ma, I know what I want to be, I know now what I want to be!" he shouted from his seat on the living room carpet, as his mother and Tilly halted their discussion in anticipation of this epiphany. "---A <u>WRITER</u>!"

As a commercial interrupted the broadcast, Mike took the opportunity to bolt into the kitchen. "A writer, Ma, that's what I want to be!" he said to the blank stare of his mother. "Last week it was an artist, Jack. What happened to the water-color paints we gotcha? I still got these pictures hangin' on the fridge. Now you want to be a writer? What are you gonna write?"

No matter. He bought a blank journal with his allowance (it's <u>not</u> a DIARY! he'd say defensively) that he carried everywhere. The journal itself was a statement. He didn't even need to write in it. But then he took an expensive pen from an assortment of pencils, markers and pens in the kitchen drawer, and there was no excuse. Stories began streaming out of him and he decided to finally bring one to school to present to his teacher. *Good idea! Maybe you'll get extra credit for it*, the family said. Okay. So, he put it into a specially designed cover of construction paper and cast-off watercolors and the teacher, Mrs. Schengel, loved it. Reading the bizarre tale aloud to the class, the story of a piece of runaway fruit creating chaos as it rolled down a steep hill, was a prideful thing. And when Mrs. Schengel, a young, attractive, high-heeled woman Mike had a terrible crush on, asked Assistant

Principal Zeppelin to come in for a repeat performance, Mike's dream was not only confirmed, but it strongly indicated that eventually marrying Mrs. Schengel was not such an out of reach goal.

As He Read The Piece Aloud, this time with absolute assurance and dramatic color, Mr. Zeppelin sat up front in one of the third-grade desks which looked all the more miniature as it wrapped about his sizeable girth, and Mrs. Schengel, perched upon her desk, dark pantyhose-covered legs which ended in those remarkably strappy shoes, on full display, Mike felt like Sinatra at the Sands. "That's a fine job, Michael, a fine job", Mr. Zeppelin exclaimed in his bloated, smiling face as he maneuvered awkwardly out of the seat. The brief adventure came to a close with Mr. Z tapping Mike's shoulder as Mrs. S kicked up her heels. "Let's have another big rrround of applause (he always stressed the width of the word "round") for young Michael, here". It was a moment.

"I guess the runaway peach thing is popular", Mike later said to his jealous schoolmates. "Who knew?"

When Mom finally came to the classroom on open school day, she found that the story in the watercolored cover was immortalized on the bulletin board, stapled upon a contact paper background and graded with *100% - extra credit!* in a red pencil. Generally used to red pencil marks only indicating corrections, Mike finally had bragging rights, particularly as the caption stated that it was an *Original story by Michael L. who wants to become a writer when he grows up*. You could do a lot worse.

It all fell apart when Hottie Schengel pulled Mom aside to complain about the harsh nature of Mike's additional stories, the ones depicting graphic beheadings and murderous fire beasts from outer space. Mom being asked about violence in the home was bound to become an issue. So, some of the luster wore off, particularly after his curt responses warranted a beating. And so, Mike went underground. Creative writing in the company of that teacher, regardless of her looking like Emma Peel, stopped, too. He feared that he'd become a marked man. Even recess carried an acute danger.

Suddenly, an intrusive, blaring ring tore through the classroom. Mrs. Schengel leapt back into her dangling high heels, grabbed her purse and directed everyone into the hallway. Maintaining size order the children moved out of the classroom, paired hand in hand, and then squatted in place, with hands over heads. Oddly, the bell continued to resound, growing in volume, a near physical assault in its intensity. The children clapped hands onto ears as Mrs. Schengel asked Mrs. Oland, "Isn't that damned bell supposed to eventually stop?!". But Mrs. Oland couldn't hear her; the harangue, ringing in advanced harmony, only trumpeted in greater and greater volume. Children began to scream as sheets of sound cast a painful swath, demanding far too much, while Mrs. Schengel, crouched in formation, prayed aloud, begging one entity or another to stop the bomb from dropping on Brooklyn.

BUT THE RINGING PERSISTED and finally woke Mike

from his near restful doze on the couch.

2:22 AM and the cool air had stiffened just enough for him

to become one with the eight-year-old facing nuclear annihilation.

He leapt up, now, with a gasp, grabbing the telephone,

more to just stop it from ringing than anything else.

His throat closed, the "hello" barely audible,

So, air space was filled by the thickened accent of Paul Filco, building manager.

"What in de hell is going on up there, Laszlo??

Were you the one threw a computer out the friggin' window?"

Mike had no response. There wasn't a proper answer.

"Goddamnit, you nuts or something?

I ain't used to complaint calls wake me up in de, in de, in de middle of night!".

Mike still had no response and the silence only egged Paul Filco further on.

"Jesus Christ, you, you, you frickin'…"

It ended up being a well-deserved beating, so to speak. But Mike knew better. Mike knew.

Mike always knew.

Punk Jazz

Razoring over, under,
Taste the bass and
Chew the battered ride cymbal which
Shimmers in the darkling.
Biting with teeth of
Cast iron and hammered sword,
The engorged heart…
Krang, riiip!
Unearth the jazz of a century in
The halls of tomorrow…
Tannng, stunnnn!
Sing out for all buried,
All taken.

Electric,
The visions unearthed beneath the
Underground,
Far below the waves of none.
Each filthy swallow of lost downtown
Is a whisper to the primal,
The noise of theory. It gets me still,

And the wind smells so strong of closure and
Tears.
I cover my wanton mouth.

Our touch is internal.
Enough to shutter the steps to finality
As the audience rapture is drowned by cries,
Matching my thirst for sounds savage and
Words of revolution.
Erased, my throat dries,
Shedding foam and dust,
And particles of past movements,
Past upheavals and distortion rebellions.
Now I await the blinding dark that comes only
With the bluest hour.

-September 6, 2021, 3:25pm

The Firefly

That breeze: it's almost there.
A near miss, it softens mid-summer air as
The city descends upon rush-hour.
4:59 and all's beginning to thread.
Slim & Slam serenade from the furthest edge of near,
Just 60 years hence but
This is still Selby's Brooklyn.

Pay no mind to the tie-up long approaching
Third Avenue,
A symphony of horns as
The tenor saxophone moans over triplets and
The rhythm guitar dances
Like a piston on Sunday morning.
A smiling from just above, largely innocent,
Melts within

My bourbon on the rocks. Look, see; the glass fogs as
The sun shifts high over the building.
THAT building,
The one on Third, that walk-up. You know.
It's across from the ghost of a theatre;

And we are ready to move in.

Harry never fades, he just resides in echoes.

On a good day, you can smell the salt air from here, the

Atlantic roaming outward, forward,

And

The borough becomes just another

Sea-faring town.

It surrounds Manhattan like a fallen idol.

-at the Brooklyn Firefly, 7/23/21, 7:55pm

The Dwindling Time

Verdant, autumn's sapling

Forges its leavening, defying,

Defying

The coming frost.

As go the leaves,

So falls the sky:

Forays without

Shadow or stone.

Night moves day, yet

Neither sun nor moon

Withstand the will of

Rising tide.

Voice of the wind

Carries the dark on

Tongues asperous

And worn.

Mark of the withering,

Face blunted in fade;

The dwindling.

The dwindling time.

-March 22, 2021, 11:12pm

The Certainty of Current

It was the sound of water drew him in. The sound of rushing water. A distant, consistent, whirring, trickling, not quite running water that stood out, demanding a presence that day.

That day he went back.

The sound, calling to him almost by name, was set far into the background of this pilgrimage, nearly gone unnoticed. But upon closer listening, it became amazingly present and clear.

Yes, yes, there it was again.

Jack cocked his head toward it, this steady flow; an aural wealth to become enraptured in, a near orchestra of sensation. Highs and lows that shimmer and dip, bubbling, humming, tickling rocks and foliage in an unmistakable fashion. A sound so complete that it, ironically, seemed staged wholly for the tourists to this sleepy little spot hidden upstate. But he wasn't a tourist, really, more of an old friend, a returning visitor with roots planted deep in those rocks and that foliage.

No, not quite running water. It was softer, more of a walk.

The *shhhhhhhhhhhhhh* of it most alluring.

He carefully moved up the street, beyond the house, the one he'd been studying since arriving in town, the one he sensed a strange familiarity with. It was hard not to stare at the house, to gaze almost through the walls, into his own visions, igniting scant memories of so long ago. But just as he considered that it would be better to move along, lest someone wonder why he peered so deeply into their home, the sound of the not quite rushing water came to him, calling. And with each step further into the shady lonesome, the faintly familiar became significantly more so.

Still.

Static.

The air about him.

Mildly cool end-of-August air that embraced his approach. The sun, not yet overhead but offering a gentle glow over this late morning, late summer scene. And it felt just right for such an adventure of solitude, a signpost guiding him to the quiet.

Traffic faded, then, as the wide avenue behind came to a halt. And he was only aware of the moment, this moment sitting squarely in the center of no time.

Moving along now, gently ahead, Jack refused to allow in the withdrawal. Too fleeting, too fragile this instant.

His steps fell silent, cautious not to touch ground too firmly.

As he tacitly moved up the road, the sound--that sound—

called out to him

with the certainty of current, the urgency singing over all but his halted breath.

He continued on as the homes which flanked his journey grew further apart. The very ground led beyond the houses and fences and little yards with trim patches of lawn, and there was a strange quietude bowing to his approach, his re-entering.

He happened upon a stretch of green with natural tree growth, the earth itself reaching upward and in embrace, acknowledging his very steps within the fold. And then suddenly a slight clearing, an opening of doors to the rushing symphony of sound.

A damp coolness poured into the air and the rushing water called out loudly now and he…

…he was taken, almost involuntarily. A newfound moist breeze, the one he could smell just before feeling on his face, fondled senses, touching with care. It drew his gaze downward… and

There lied the Brook.

The cool water flowed clean as he stood on its bank, at remembrance's rise. Jack reveled in the moment: lost childhood hours through years erased. Building dams, catching frogs and minnows, listening to the rustle of the leaves. And the movement of the water, voices in the current. So cold, so clear, so welcoming, this tiny mountain stream.

The foothills of the Catskills burst free here and meet the sky in hushed reflection, offering sonority in the wells of silence. So, he stood on its muddy bank, eyes shut, becoming one with the sudden memories without once rupturing the special, secret moment.

Shhhhhhhhhhhhhhh.

The visions came and went and came again, forming and melting before closed eyes.

Shhhhhhhhhhh…………

The water trickled along like an endless, timeless whisper,

Reciting verses of simplicity and age.

He breathed in deeply, trying for all he could to absorb this re-foundation. It held on briefly and then, without warning, the drone of distant traffic crept back in.

Sounds down road came to forefront, the noise of this day, and a loud car radio taunted as it raced the avenue.

And the moment fell mislaid.

And his private foray was closed.

Now he stood, an outsider without destination. Jack peered up into the trees overhead, hesitating before turning to depart. He reached for one further cleansing breath, hoping, fruitlessly, to steal back the seconds.

But he was already gone.

Again.

From Empty to Away

He'd been reduced to staring numbly at the television. Long, this lasted long, augmenting as he diminished. The quips, funny voices and Dad jokes long forgotten, his clipped street baritone had become a hoarse, rustling tenor. One of scant endurance.

Over time, the condition greedily advanced, overtaking the man in his most weakened state.

We spoke; he looked back, empty. NOT not just blank but removed. An erasure.

The young doctor, all wide-eyed, raised brow and white lab coat.

The old man, his patient, held his eyes tightly shut as we spoke over.

He HE LOOKED looked so fragile, I thought. Child-like from this angle.

It happened, this shifting of roles, so irrevocably.

The doctor began speaking with his hands, rapidly explaining, but I

I was drawn into the background, blurred by arhythmic beeps, buzzers, and overhead announcementsThe doctor, nearly clarifying his points,something about

CT results,left frontal lobeParietal lobe,andandparietal and"Do you have further questions?", he asked *percussively*, the last,

That last syllableSyllable carrying

with it a leap

of nearly one full oc-oct-

ocTAVE.

…And a familiar darkness strained upward, gripping my throatmy as father lay nearly still. Small.   So small, very small. Hollowed.

AND THEN I was pulled into the hocus at ER's entrance:

another bus in the bay, *bus in the bay*, gurney rushing,rushing in, passing me, rushing, nurses with crash cart and //

Looking long enough, I can see him go from empty to away.

Empty to away.

As white lab coat faded into powder blue curtains, I rolled this phrase silently over tongue and lips, a whisper softer even than my father's. Empty to away. Barely a mouthing. How profound, how perfectly simple, it's immobile. An ebb, a melt, a razing, a striking. An erasure. Nowhere left to go.

My father stirred. "Hey, Dad, are how you doing?"
He didn't look back this time.

I stared into his face, absorbing it. Before it's away. And my thoughts traveled inward, recalling childhood visits to the home of my father's father. His vision had eroded, ravaged by diabetes and the stoic little man with bristly gray stubble said: "Johnny, c'mere. I wanna look atcha".

"Look at me, Grampa? What do you mean?"

The answer lingers over these decades. Holding me carefully by the shoulders, from his spot on the plastic-covered couch, Grandpa mournfully said, "I want ta look atcha so I can remember. So, I don't forget whatcha look like".

The erasure is always chasing us down, bringing us to away. To away.

Our prize is in the enduring.

-September 17, 2021, 11:05pm

Union Square East

No, no, he wasn't really going anywhere,

Not anywhere, really, but

The riled man felt the need to

Hasten

Through

The thicket of

Subterranean

New York.

The crush that had once been relegated to "rush hour"

Now exists across a several-hour span, twice daily.

Here, below the buckling streets, the cluster never breathes.

He looked onto the emerging wall of walkers,

Aimless walkers, and,

With chin low, maneuvered through the crowd with certain urgency. The tunnels twist Escher-like from one end of 14th Street to the other, so one must stay ahead of the fray. One must stay ahead of the fray. One must.

Too hot to rush, but it was the only way through it

If he didn't want to wait for the shuttle.

He didn't.

Just above, ropey condensation gathered on the aged tunnel ceiling,

Defying gravity,

Balancing over the heads of the unsuspecting mass.

And further down, a young busker, eyes near shut,

Played jazz guitar through a micro-amp by the dull grey metal sign:

TO UNION SQUARE >

The driven man obeyed

As the chords of "Brilliant Corners"

Became of the surrounding din,

Foot-steps fused electric strings…

…Swerving, swerving now around a group of overtly blonde tourists strolling stately while the senior-most clutched a map in death grip, the harried man found himself in the path of a new thicket of oncoming zombies.

As the throng momentarily subsided, he whirled around

And onward

And beyond, trying to regain lost time and

He nearly ran into the tall, bearded elder,

In a tin hat,

Red-faced,

Leaning against the tiled wall,

Preaching REDEMPTION to

an invisible congregation

in the soupy haze.

But the man whizzes by,

Sore afraid to weaken pace…

Surfing a wave of commuters rushing to the oncoming # 4,

He leapt toward a shaft of golden sunlight,

Some say charismatically guided.

Now,

Now rushing through the turnstile intently,

He bolts up the steps and

Outside,

Out,

Into beckoning day.

The man looks over Union Square's cavalcade.

Vendors and

Artists,

Tourists and breaking workers,

The homeless and

New wealth, the

Button-down luxury

That once housed New Yorkers.

The stilled masses line up, hiding from

Burgeoning August,

Along the park's edge, breathing in the shade.

He--briskly now--steps over NYU students

In parallel play

On concrete stairs,

Juggling overpriced coffee,

Laughing aloud, charmed, as he,

As he falls to the sidewalk

Toward the relative comfort

Of chaos,

Union Square East.

And the song of rushing traffic

Swells to delicious cacophony

Over broiling

blacktop.

The Turning of California Tony

Shortly after Nicky Lustig moved into the 3-story walk-up on West 39th, he married Lucille. Everyone knew Lucille: you couldn't possibly miss the clinging skirts sheathing a length of leg. But none of the old gang had dared approach her as they stood daily at their corner post.

"She thinks who she is".

But as disturbed as the boys were by getting nowhere with the vexing looker, nothing fueled their ire more than the knowledge that Nicky, the newsstand owner's son, had landed her. Nicky. Goddamned Nicky. "Frickin' little shit", they'd say. When Nicky would come home from work, they tried to stare him down, but he never gave it a second thought.

"Fuck you, Nicky, and every shit that looks like you".

Much to the chagrin of the corner boys, it wasn't long before Lucille's figure had changed considerably, and she'd traded in tight skirt for maternity dress. Soon, Nicky was giving out cigars and buying rounds of beer for the old gang. After that, all was well on 11th Avenue, particularly once the children, cigars and rounds began arriving quite regularly. Besides, none could even recall when Lucille hadn't been pregnant.

IT WAS ALWAYS KNOWN AS AN INORDINATELY QUIET BUILDING. Finster, the landlord, lived on the first floor. He hit the sack early every night, right after turning down his hearing aid. When Nicky first took the apartment, he'd only run into his upstairs neighbor, known as California Tony, on rare occasions on the staircase or by the mailboxes in the lobby. Older than the neighborhood guys, employed on the night-shift at the bottle factory, California spent little time socializing. He had a thing for silence. In daylight, he only ventured out for coffee or over to Nicky's father's newsstand on 41st to buy a pack of Chesterfields. His salt-and-pepper hair, slicked into a tall

DA, carried the scent of hair lacquer down the stairs and out the door, along with very stale smoke.

Working the midnight-to-8 as he did, California slept during the day—or tried to. As the noise level grew just beneath him, it was matched by a stewing anger. The din, multiplying every nine months or so, swirled into his exhausted daytime dream state. Nothing helped.

When Andrea, the third, was born, he'd simply had enough. Babies wailing, toddlers running and fighting, children's singalong records on the hi-fi, Captain Kangaroo and cartoons blaring on the damned set. All of this just as he was trying to get to sleep. Stories spread of California in boxer shorts, sleep mask hanging loosely about his neck, screaming down from his window, "Lady, I gotta get ta sleep!", he'd shout. "I wuyk nights!"

"Nicky, that guy's crazy, I tell ya", Lucille increasingly warned her husband. Attempts to work things out with California went bad, and then the two began to argue horribly. Even old Finster heard bits of the commotion, just before he'd turn down his hearing aid. It got ugly from there.

SO WRONGED DID CALIFORNIA TONY FEEL by the trebly, troubling voices beneath, that he took to rolling his bowling ball back and forth on his hardwood living room floor. Each evening, over the young family's heads.

This rumbling torment went on during dinner and continued into the night. Whenever there was nothing good on TV, California persisted three, four hours at a stretch. Over and over, the old 16-pound Brunswick was unleased over uncarpeted walkways like it was taking down a spare in alley 9 of the Bowl-a-Rama.

He was only inspired more by Nicky's hysterical poking at his ceiling with a broom within showers of screamed curses. This nightly ritual usually ended with California, about 11:30, dropping the bowling ball hard onto his floor, a bellow of ungodly thunder. The crack and quake of it tickled him, but he only reveled in the muffled shouts rising upward.

Any notion of armistice was now futile. The fighting continued through the birth of the twins, during which time, Nicky decided they needed to move. He packed up Lucille, little Debbie, Gerard and Andrea along with Mikey and Ikey, and drove off to their new home, a nice set of rooms over on 6th Avenue. But Nicky remained unable to forget the torment.

With the old gang helping to unload the truck, Nicky knew he must make right the wrong. “I’ll be home in a minute, hon”, he shouted to Lucille as he was getting into his car. “Just going out for cigarettes”, he said slipping a jack-handle up his denim sleeve.

Arriving in front of the old walk-up, Nicky parked off the corner and

quietly entered the small lobby. The building was hushed,

asleep in the absence of the flurry

that had been.

He carefully ascended the creaky staircase, soft-shoeing beyond Finster’s apartment (he was by now out like a light) and then his old vacant flat. Nicky moved upward, beyond the landing and up to the third-floor front. Where his nemesis lay sound asleep.

It was hot and California Tony’s apartment door was slightly ajar, the way he’d often kept it before the fights began. “Now I have him, the bastard”, Nicky thought from his perch, crouching at the top of the stairs.

He slipped the jack-handle out of his sleeve, gripping it in both fists, and crept toward California’s lair. The smell of cigarettes clung to everything. And through it, there remained the scent of spray-freeze hair lacquer.

Nicky elbowed the door open and, holding his breath, leapt into the apartment. As his feet landed on the mildly scarred hardwood, the reverberation of an empty apartment couldn't be mistaken for any other sound. A pair of keys sat on the kitchen counter with a forwarding address in Encino.

He was alone but for the billowing smoke.

Starless

The Stillwell Avenue station, late-night, late winter.

Starless.

The elevated platform offers

No shelter from insistent frost.

The tireless aroma of candy and deep-fry hang in the wind,

Splintered, now, like peeling paint.

Out of season, on such a night, Coney Island is a solitary place.

Distant, remote, forlorn.

The amusement park felled silent, a snap-shot in time,

Its carousel horses stare blankly, mouths agape.

Locked down rollercoasters and shuttered crazy houses look back,

Mockingly. The party has been over for months, come again next summer…

The roar of the 11:45 to Manhattan barrels into the station,

Tearing into the blackened sky as

The seats on the long-dormant Wonder Wheel rock,

Ever so briefly, with tormented excitement.

-Commonwealth Bar, Brooklyn, April 20, 2019, 12:58AM

Coda

In the small of a darkened room lighted by laptop

He sat.

A light snowfall pelted the windows as he typed,

Racing the calendar's turning.

The space, chilled, work, faster…

Scores of scenarios they came,

Fettered words, scattered notes and whispers.

Unending, this day, it took on dusk and bled the hours.

Then, it began.

Muted trumpets clouding memory as

Guy Lombardo's saxophones hovered just overhead.

Heavy on vibrato.

Look, see: the Waldorf's four-color avatar on his kitchen wall,

Dancing a waltz from hours within.

The muse sparks bright but realized in haze.

The fading percepts of past passerby,

Spiritual exceptions, glistenings in gold.

The pen awakens, cleaving the soul…

Raven, the arcane night filled the room.
The candor of glare leaving eyes radiant.

And soon, a shouting exultation and
Serenades of ratchets and horns expressing holiday air.
And fireworks lit the skies over Manhattan.

He ran to the window, then, tossing it open,
A hand to the throngs, welcoming the adulation.
The cheering rose in its pitch and volume, and
The peoples' embrace, tearful kisses of joy.
And he,
He, shredding the dark turned one with
Night's sky.

So smeared, the rainbows of ink,
Saturation to the vivid.

###

ACKNOWLEDGEMENTS

"The Night Leonard Cohen Died" was originally published in
Love Love #5, March 2022

"Those Enduring Neon Moments" was originally published in
The Avenue journal, February 2022

"Night for Day: 11 and 9" was premiered on the *Jazz Just After Dark* radio show (MakerParkRadio.nyc), September 10, 2022, read by Pietaro with trumpet by Mac Gollehon

"The Turning of California Tony" was originally published
Ovunque Siamo, vol 3, Number 3, 2020

"Union Square East" was originally published on
The Cultural Worker blog, 2018

Many thanks to Uncollected Press/Raw Art Review editors for believing in
A Bleeding in Black Leather.

About the Author

John Pietaro is a writer, poet, spoken word artist and musician from Brooklyn, NY. Recent publications include *The Mercer Stands Burning: Night Poems* (Atmosphere Press, 2020), and chapbook *Smoke Rings* (New Masses Media, 2019). Columnist/critic of *The NYC Jazz Record*, Pietaro is a contributing arts reporter to *PleaseKillMe, The Wire* (UK), *Z, Sensitive Skin, AllAboutJazz, The Nation, The Village Sun, CounterPunch, People's World, TruthOut* , *Fashion Arts* and others.

Further credits include multipe entries in the upcoming edition of *The Encyclopedia of the American Left* (Verso, 2023), as well as poetry or fiction for journals *Love Love* (Paris), *The Avenue, Lucent Dreaming, Heroes Are Gangleaders Giantology, Headline Press, Rye, Genre: Urban Arts, Ovunque Siamo, Harbinger Asylum,* and International Human Rights Arts Festival press. Pietaro also penned contemporary proletarian fiction collection *Night People & Other Tales of Working New York* (2013) and contributed a chapter to Paul Buhle and Harvey Pekar's *SDS: A Graphic History* (Hill & Wang, 2007). His work has also beern seen in various anthologies.

Pietaro directs The Brecht Lives! Festival, among other events, hosts radio shows 'Beneath the Underground' (WFMU/Sheena's Jungle Room) and 'Jazz Just After Dark' (makerparkradio.nyc), and fronts post-punk jazz/poetry ensemble the Red Microphone, ESP-Disk artists. The band's latest album, named for this literary collection, is set for a late 2022 launch. In 2021 they released *And I Became of the Dark*. The Red Microphone earlier collaborated in studio and on stage with poet Amina Baraka, who also performed Pietaro's "Her Side of the Road" as a dramatic reading in 2018.

As a percussionist, multi-instrumentalist and/or spoken word artist, Pietaro's worked with many artists including Allen Ginsberg, Pete Seeger, Amina Baraka, Karl Berger, Steve Dalachinsky, Nora Guthrie, Erika Dagnino, Ras Moshe, Puma Perl, Warren Smith, Ingrid Sertso, Ngoma Hill, Ray Korona, and Paul Buhle.

Literature as a weapon for social change, liberation and expression is at the core of John Pietaro's arts philosophy. A primary influence remains the literary Left of the 1910s-1980s, here and abroad: the revolutionists, cutural workers, muckrakers, avant gardists, Beats, free jazzers, outsiders, and punk rockers, night dwellers all.

Website: **JohnPietaro.com** ***Blog:*** **TheCulturalWorker.blogspot.com**

www.ingramcontent.com/pod-product-compliance
Lightning Source LLC
LaVergne TN
LVHW090538110826
845146LV00003B/1158

* 9 7 9 8 9 8 6 7 2 4 3 0 0 *